Trainir

GW01191216

L.M. Mountford

Copyright © 2021 by L.M. Mountford

All rights reserved. No part of this publication may be reproduced, distributed or transmitted in any form or by any means, including photocopying, recording, or other electronic or mechanical methods, without the prior written permission of the publisher, except in the case of brief quotations embodied in critical reviews and certain other noncommercial uses permitted by copyright law. For permission requests, write to the publisher, addressed "Attention: Permissions Coordinator," at the address below.

L.M. Mountford
United Kingdom
Training Tracey

Published 2021
By The Lord of Lust Publications

Publisher's Note: This is a work of fiction. Names, characters, places, and incidents are a product of the author's imagination. Locales and public names are sometimes used for atmospheric purposes. Any resemblance to actual people, living or dead, or to businesses, companies, events, institutions, or locales is completely coincidental.

Edited by readabit: Copy Editing and Proofreading Services Est 2018
L.M. Mountford – 2nd Ed.
ISBN: 978-1-913945-38-1

THE LORD OF LUST PUBLICATIONS

About the Author

A self-confessed Tiger fanatic, L.M. Mountford was born and raised in England, first in the town of Bridgewater, Somerset, before later moving to the city of Gloucester where he currently resides. A fully qualified and experienced Scuba Diver, he has travelled across Europe and Africa diving wrecks and seeing the wonders of the world.

He started writing when he was 14. Under the pseudonym Dark Inferno, he has written more than thirty Fanfiction stories.

Other Titles by L.M. Mountford

Collections

Deliciously Sinful Liaisons
Sweet Temptations Box Set
Just a Number

The Sweet Temptations Series

The Babysitter
The Boss's Daughter

Just Friends Series

Just Once

Broken Heart Series

Broken

Stand Alone Titles

Uncovered
Serving the Senator
Together in Sydney
Blood Lust
Reckless
Tequila Sunset
Forbidden Desire

Training Tracey

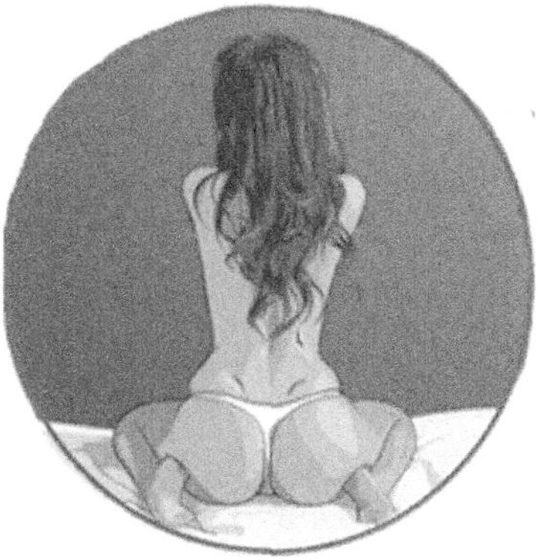

THE LORD OF LUST

L.M. MOUNTFORD

L.M Mountford
THE LORD OF LUST PUBLICATIONS

Chapter ONE

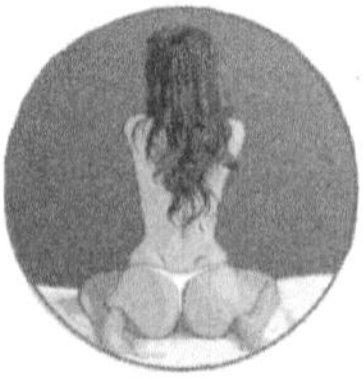

Amanda Burton sighed happily as she pulled her sleek Jaguar XK convertible into her driveway. Nothing beat a drive with the top down after a long day showing potential buyers all around the west country to look at houses. Even the inevitable paperwork that followed was remedied by a sunset drive. Now all she needed was a glass of wine or two, a long soak in a hot tub, and she'd kick off the weekend with a few rounds of much-needed sex with her husband.

The air was heavy with a perfume of wildflowers and far to the west, the sun had slipped behind the rolling green horizon, turning from blue to a deep lavender before the oncoming wall of night. Killing the engine, she stepped out of the vehicle. Not bothering to put the XK's roof back up or collect her briefcase from the boot, she walked up the path to her home whilst fishing in her pocket for her keys.

The door slid inwards as she brought her key up to the lock.

Strange. Stepping back, Amanda looked up. All the lights were off. A quick glance around confirmed hers was the only car in the drive. She shrugged it off. *The girls must have forgotten to lock up on their way out.* It certainly wouldn't be the first time her daughter, Camila, or one of her friends had left the door ajar. Amanda was just glad they'd moved down to Ashcott when they did. God only knows what might have happened if they still lived at the old house in Hereford.

Say what you want about remote villages in the middle of nowhere. They certainly had a much lower crime rate than cities and towns. And the commute had its perks.

Shutting the door firmly and securely behind her, Amanda shrugged off her jacket.

She froze, ears pricked and searching. She could hear something, faint and indistinct like a voice lost in the wind.

Her curiosity peaked, Amanda looked around, trying to figure out its origin, half expecting to find Camila on the phone to one of her friends. *Upstairs. It's coming from upstairs.*

Stealthily as a jackrabbit, Amanda ascended the wooden stairs and made her way along the landing, the sound growing louder with every step. She stopped outside her daughter's room. Grabbing the handle to open the door she suddenly had an idea and instead sunk to her knees before placing one hand against the side of the door. She brushed a stray lock of her dishevelled hair away from her ear.

Not so very long ago, Amanda would probably have just barged right in all guns blazing, but recently Camila had been growing increasingly secretive and prickly where her room and personal space was concerned. She wouldn't take kindly to someone, specifically her mother, bursting in unannounced. Amanda had a very good idea what was going on.

Barely a month ago, Camila had found herself her first real boyfriend.

She listened intently, her ear pressed against the wood, for any sound coming from within the room that might explain her daughter's absence. From her own experiences as a hormone-driven teenager, she fully expected to hear the hurried whispers and scattered moans that always indicated a passionate nookie session. However, she couldn't hear much of anything except for a very faint sobbing.

Finally, curiosity and parental concern got the better of her. Lightly pressing her palm against the wood, she silently forced the door open a crack.

Camila's room was one of the smallest in the house and was lightly lit by the low glow of her bedside lamp, casting it in a comfortable light that revealed its surprisingly neat and tidy furnishings. Taking a second to let her eyes adapt to the low light, Amanda immediately looked to the large queen size that was situated at the back of the rectangular room. She was surprised to find, not her daughter, but Camila's friend, Tracey, curled in a weeping ball.

Amanda threw open the door and hurried across the room to the sobbing girl and pulled her close. Without hesitation or a word of protest, the girl accepted the hug and cried into her blouse.

"Tracey… What's wrong honey?" She asked gently, running her hand through her waves of golden hair, trying to sooth the distressed eighteen-year-old.

Tracey Fox never cried. In all the years Amanda had known her she'd watched her grow and flourish. For as long as she had been Camila's BFF, she had never cried. Even as a girl, despite her wide eyes and deceptive, doll-like innocence, she had looked at life with the tenacity of a bulldog. What could have happened to turn her into such a wreck? And where was-

"C-Camila…" Amidst the sobs, the girl's voice sounded choked and almost inaudible, but Amanda heard the name all the same. It was like a cold wash down her spine. She didn't push her, however, but continued trying to soothe her with soft words.

When her sobs finally began to subside, Tracey looked up at her with a stranger's face and a look in her eye that made the older woman want to cry out in horror. Gone was the rosy-cheeked, bright-eyed girl. Now, she was only a shadow, a ghost of her former self, pale with puffy eyes that still freely leaked tears. Amanda felt her throat tighten and a pain stab her chest. Without thinking, she put both arms around the girl and held her close.

"W-we were watching T.V. Jeremy ..." Tracey seemed to be on the verge of fresh tears at the mention of Camila's boyfriend and Amanda felt a sudden surge of wrath towards the boy who now dominated so much of her daughter's life. "He came round. He'd been drinking and..."

"Go on, honey don't worry, you can tell me. What happened?"

"He pulled Camila into his lap and started making remarks about us here all alone. She didn't say anything. Then he said something, suggested we play together. I thought he was out of his mind, but she only laughed and said, said it could be fun."

"She did what!"

"I said no, but Jeremy, he wouldn't listen. He started grabbing his... himself through his jeans, stroking it so we could see... Camila, she was tugging on my arm, trying to get me to come closer. I-I told them I wasn't interested, so they both got angry. They ca-called me a prude and started joking about how I was still a virgin. Finally, Jeremy... called me a frigid...cock teasing bitch!"

"No!"

Tracey nodded, tears flowing freely once again. "He said I wasn't worth the effort of getting hard for, then said they were leaving and Camila...she... she...."

"Shh- shh, it's okay sweetheart, it's okay". The damn was well and truly broken now, so Amanda did what she could to sooth the girl once more through the babble of unintelligible sobs. Amanda couldn't believe what she was hearing. Of course, she'd known that both Camila and Tracey, despite both being beautiful, curvy young women, had had trouble with boys growing up.

Neither she nor Mark liked Jeremy very much. There was an arrogance behind his movie-star good looks and smouldering eyes and a swagger that just didn't sit right with Amanda.

Her husband, however, had a much more eloquent way of putting it. *The boy's a cock.*

A threesome, really! How could he even suggest such a thing in her bloody house? To think her own daughter could turn on her friend for that little shit, of all people. Amanda made a note to personally cut his cock off and feed it to him if he ever came near Camila again.

"What's wrong with me?" The question came out of the blue and at first Amanda wasn't sure Tracey had said anything.

"It's okay honey, it's okay. There's nothing wrong- "

"Then why?" she snapped, her body rigid. "It's just sex, everyone does it! So why, why did the thought of him touching me-"

"You're not ready, that's all it is."

"But I am ready. I want to. But I just…can't." The word came out as a sigh and all the aggression and tension in her body seemed to leave her with her confession.

"Trust me, when you meet the right one, and you're both ready, you will. And it'll be worth the wait."

Slowly, Tracey looked up to meet Amanda's gaze. "Was that the way it was for you?"

"Yes."

"Was it Mr Burton?"

"Yes." Amanda couldn't help but smile, remembering how it had felt to be young and caught up in the spell of first love. And then, noticing the way Tracey appeared to be hanging on her every word, she had an idea. "Is there someone?"

"Well… yes- no, no, I shouldn't be telling you- I- I have to go!" Cheeks tinged pink with embarrassment, Tracey wheeled, but Amanda seized her arm before she could make it off the bed.

"Hey! Wait a second. Come on, you can tell me..."

"No, it's embarrassing."

"Is he good looking?"

"Yes."

"Is he a boy at Strode?"

"No."

"Oh…Do I know him? Does he live nearby?"

"Y-yes."

"Close?"

"Very." Tracey was looking at the floor and seemed to be studying the plain simple carpet with all the scrutiny of a master architect as her cheeks burned crimson and she twisted the bedspread with white knuckles.

Was she afraid? What did Tracey have to be afraid of? She'd gushed over boys with her before. One of the perks of being a *cool* parent was that your daughter's friends came to you for advice. Tracey had been Camila's best friend since they started secondary school, so she already knew the types of boys she was attracted to-

Then the penny dropped. "Ah. I see."

Tracey stiffened, and she had to force herself to meet Amanda's eyes. She looked like a deer caught in the headlights. "I'm so sorry, I never meant-"

"It's fine sweetie. I understand." She had caught Tracey sneaking peeks before, but she had always dismissed it. With his tall, broad build, thick waves of sandy blonde hair, cobalt eyes, and a biostructure that would make a stone mason weep with envy, it came as no surprise to Amanda that her husband caught considerable amounts of attention from the women around him. Why should this hormone-wracked teen be any different? He was a very good-looking man. What red-blooded woman wouldn't enjoy the odd bit of voyeur pleasure. It was half the reason Amanda, though not prone to jealousy, enjoyed taking every opportunity to flaunt herself on his arm whenever they went out. *Marking her territory*, as he would put it. She forced a reassuring smile. "And you don't have to worry about a thing…"

"What do you mean?"

Amanda put a comforting hand on her shoulder. "Tell me honey, have you ever heard of *The Lifestyle*?"

"Y-you mean swinging?"

She nodded an affirmative. "That's one word for it, yes."

Tracey nervously licked her lips, the pink of her tongue darting out across her soft peach-coloured mouth as she tried to find the words. "So…you're? I mean, you and Mr Burton are...have?"

"Swung?" Amanda offered, bringing an adorable tinge of pink to the girls otherwise flawless, milky, pale skin. "Yes, well we've never been, what you'd call practising, but some old friends of ours in Hereford were. They've always been very open about it but were careful to make sure it never became an issue. They understood not everyone agreed with their lifestyle choice. Well, over drinks one night we got to talking. A little too much wine, the odd touch here, a flirtatious remark there. One thing just sort of lead to another. It never became a regular thing, but we'd go around now and again. They introduced us to other practising couples they thought would be a good fit for us. Some worked. Others, not so much. These days though we only really partake in the occasional long weekend *retreats*."

"But what about Camila?" Tracey cut in. "She's okay with you two doing this? I can't believe it. I'm her best friend and she never said anything about you two being into any of this to me."

"Because she doesn't know. No one around here does. It's none of their business."

"But you want me to- "

"Sweetie, I don't want you to do anything. I understand this is a lot to take in and if talking about it makes you uncomfortable then forget it. We're not talking about joining a cult, you don't have to do anything you don't want to, and if you want to stop you only have to say. It won't make any difference to how we feel about you."

"But if I-" Tracey cut in, her voice panicked as if she was suddenly afraid the offer might be withdrawn at any minute. "I am. If I'm okay with... with everything, you'd be willing to, to let me, to let me and Mr Burton..."

"Why not? It's nothing we haven't done before." Amanda gave the girl's shoulder a reassuring squeeze and leaned down to press a soft kiss to her lips. "And besides, a girl's first time should be special, with someone who knows what he's doing. And Mark is very, very *good*."

"But what if he doesn't, he might not want to-"

"What if he doesn't want to be your first, or doesn't want to fuck the brains out of a hot little eighteen-year-old?" Her full rosy lips arched into an unmistakably feline smirk. "Leave that to me."

Chapter TWO

"You want me to do what!" Mark thundered, all but spraying his tea across the living room wall.

"Now don't overreact. All I said was I want you to go upstairs and have sex with our daughter's best friend." Amanda countered, remaining perfectly calm and collected even as tingles raced down to the pit of her stomach.

"Overreact?" Lost for words and battling to keep calm, Mark took off his glasses and began to clean the lenses with the hem of his shirt, fruitlessly rubbing at an invisible smudge. "Okay, let me see if I've got this straight. You come home from work to find Tracey crying upstairs after having some sort of fight with Cam about her still being a virgin, and you come away from that thinking that the best thing we can do to help is me fucking her?" Sliding his glasses back onto the bridge of his nose, he shot his wife a scrutinising stare. "Did I miss anything?" His question dripped sarcasm.

Amanda frowned. "I'm serious, Mark."

"You are, aren't you?" Mark groaned, slumping all the way back into his chair and rubbing the bridge of his nose. "Fuck me".

"Later dear. And please, watch your language." Amanda countered, sitting down beside him on the leather sofa. A half amused, half reassuring smile tugging at the corner of her mouth.

He sighed and put a hand on her thigh, giving her a reassuring squeeze through the fabric of her pencil skirt. "Hun, you know I would do anything for Tracey. She's practically one of the family. I just think taking her virginity is asking a little much." That was putting it mildly. The whole idea was crazy, yet he'd seen that look in her eyes before and knew she was convinced and set on this path. A blunt approach wouldn't work here. For now, he needed to be diplomatic to make her see sense.

As if she could read his thoughts, however, Amanda slid down off the sofa.

"Amanda?" He warned, his eyes drinking in the site of her crawling provocatively between his legs and a delicate hand reaching out to tug on the fly of his trousers. "Stop. Are you crazy? Tracey's just up- oh!"

Looking up at him, Amanda smiled and pulled his awakening cock from his trousers. "Oh, I don't remember that bothering you at the Christmas party last year." Then, holding his legs open with her elbows, she teased his tip with flicks of her tongue, before licking long trails down his shaft, moving from the tip to the base and vice versa.

"Tha-that's because you-you-oh fuck." The protest died in a long moan as lush lips enveloped him, sucking him into the damp cavity of her mouth, her tongue pressing against his velvet flesh and teeth scraping over the glands.

"Now back to the subject of Tracey." Amanda pronounced around him, the vibrations of each syllable shivering down his shaft, making his fingers bite a white-knuckled grip into the leather. It was a sudden rush of pleasure to his system and all Mark could do to vocalize his pleasure was to release a series of long, low grunts and moans.

He fought his immediate desires however and managed to gasp "Let's not, not now."

"Okay dear, let's not *talk,*" and Amanda promptly pulled back from his rigid arousal and wiped the corner of her mouth "Not now..."

It never ceased to amaze Amanda how Mark, whose mind had been clouded by lust mere seconds ago, could become so alert so suddenly- a point that was very well proven by the way he so quickly lifted himself up to look at her as he exclaimed "No! No...it's alright dear. We can talk...we can talk about anything you want to."

Men, so easy. All a girl needs to know is which button to press.

"So...are you ready to hear me out?" She asked, before mouthing his crown, sweeping her tongue around and around, resuming her oral assault full force. Mark tried to respond but all that came out was another long moan. Instead, he just nodded, vigorously.

Inwardly grinning like a Cheshire cat that just caught a big fat canary, Amanda closed one hand around his shaft and began softly jacking him, just to make sure she had his complete attention. "Dear, do you recall how difficult it was for me to feel comfortable with you, you know... *intimately,* when we started dating?"

With Mark's nod, Amanda pressed on.

"Well, Tracey is in that same place now more than ever. She's confused and scared and feels like everyone around her is pressuring her to take that next step. She needs someone she feels comfortable around, who knows what's he's doing, to take her by the hand and show her how wonderful sex can be."

It was a dual assault. Her attentions igniting a fire in his veins. Her words conjuring up visions of Tracey spread out beneath him, her supple body, full and bountiful, writhing and arching in sweet ecstasy. Excited to the point of delirium, he could only shake his head and splutter a protest. "No…ah…what about- oh God… Ca-Camila?"

Amanda's fingers flexed, tightening almost to the point of pain. "What about her?"

"Tracey's her best friend, I…can't…it's wrong!" he managed to muster between moans, his wife's hand steadily picking up speed, pumping him, driving him insane. Mark knew that if he didn't hold on, the pleasure his wife was creating would push him over the edge.

"It's none of her business. Cam and that asshole started all this by proposing that they have some sort of twisted threesome." She was making progress and now all she needed to do was give him that final push. "Besides, this is nothing we haven't done before."

Mark seized a fist full of her hair, tugging and twisting, but when he spoke, his voice was perfectly calm. "I thought we agreed never to talk about that."

"I know, but I miss it baby. I miss watching you fuck. Watching you use and take what you want and turn those women into babbling sex-crazed wantons. It gets me so… hot." She consumed as much as she could, sliding her mouth down his shaft in a tight seal, taking half of him in one go then hollowing her cheeks as she pulled back. "Don't you want to feel those soft lips…wrapped around your hard cock…" Wet slurps punctured each of her impassioned expletives as she repeated the long pull, her head bobbing faster and faster. The imagery she was conjuring made her clit throb and liquid heat pooled in her belly. "Feel her tight little pussy quivering, clenching…as you watch our daughter's best friend's big tits bouncing as she rides your dick-"

"I'll do it…" He had her on her back before she knew it. He used his grip on her hair to pull her off him and to her feet, before launching her across the sofa. She bounced with the first contact, but then he was on her, devouring the lips that only moments before had been wrapped around his cock. "Later."

With one hand cupping her bottom, the other was kneading her breast through her shirt. He began the delicate and most practised art of toying with her body, working her into a frenzy that had weak whimpers flowing from her very soul. The urge to surrender to his hunger was as intoxicating as honey wine, sweet and so delicious. It took all the power she possessed to wake herself from the pleasurable haze and to gather her wits.

Amanda quickly did the only thing she could think of.

She reached down and fisted the *root* of his desire. "Bad Boy."

Chapter THREE

This was crazy.

Mark hesitated on the landing, just outside Camila's door, the weight of what he was about to do resting around his neck like the hangman's noose. What the fuck are you doing?

He carried on regardless, slowly turning the handle to his errant daughter's room and opening the wooden door. He could do this. Amanda was right, this wasn't the first time they had indulged in The Lifestyle. That point did little to distract him from his nerves, however. Experienced or not, it wasn't every day that one's own wife commissions you to fuck your daughter's best friend, and a virgin of all things. It was a daunting prospect and one that carried with it all the pressures of the first time you have sex. And even though he knew he should relax, the thought made him feel like a virgin all over again.

He was just trying to quell the feeling when he heard the soft, alluring moans from within, turning his still hard cock to steel in his trousers.

The room was lit only by the dim glow of the bedside lamp, the soft illumination creating a sensual atmosphere.

Tracey was stretched out across the queen size, one hand fondling her breasts through her top, slender fingers pinching a hardened nipple. The other was hidden from his view, having slid beneath the waistband of her jeans all the way to the wrist. He could just make out the outline of her knuckles moving beneath the crotch, coaxing those sexy little sounds.

“Please Mr Burton, take me. I want to feel you in me...”

Dark cloudy eyes opened wide as they wandered from the tantalizing dance of her fingers, up over her alluring bosom, to finally settle on her angelic face, shrouded in strands of dirty gold. With her cheeks flushed and eyes half-lidded, she had the look of a siren basking on the rocks, luring ships of desperate sailors to their demise and ruin on the rocks. But what a way to go…

"Mr Burton," Tracey moaned, pinching her clit viciously between her thumb and forefinger, then sliding another one of her long fingers deep within her creamy slit. “Oh God…Mr Burton…You’re so big, Oh God…Mr Burton…Oh, Mr Burton…Oh…Ooh…Mr Burton! I’m cumming! I’m cumming! I’m…” The mini-orgasm hit her in waves and Tracey’s voice died away, lost on the tide as she climaxed on her hand, tiny ripples washing over her with increasing intensity, then ebbing away just as quickly.

Panting, she brought her fingers up to her lips, each digit shiny with her desire, and began licking them clean.

Tracey couldn't explain it, couldn't understand what had come over her. She had been so nervous.

She couldn't believe it was going to happen and was so afraid it might all turn out to be a dream, that at any moment she might wake up to cold reality. Finally, the one person she had been craving for years was going to be hers. After so long, all her dreams were about to come true and she would lose her v-card, and to Mr Burton, her best friend's father.

The idea was so deliciously forbidden that a tide of heat had washed over her. Her mind had flooded with images of Camila's dad on the beach. The family had taken her and a few of Camila's other friends with them to Weston-Super-Mare in the summer holidays. His large muscular body stripped bare and swimming shorts that teased the outline of his hard cock whenever they were wet.

Before really registering what she was doing, her hand had undone the fastenings of her jeans. Her thumb lightly brushed against her clit and a low moan slipped past her lips as warmth spread through her. She began playing with her clit, rolling it between her fingers before moaning louder as she tentatively slipped a finger inside her entrance. Lost in the moment, her world melted away like chocolate, and Tracey gave herself over to the pleasure.

There was a creaking sound and Tracey's eyes immediately snapped into focus to discover Mark standing in the doorway, leaning leisurely against the timber frame, arms crossed, watching her with the eyes of a hungry wolf.

"Mr Burton!" She exclaimed. Embarrassed, she tried to cover herself with the quilt.

Mark only smirked, staying silent except for the rustling of his clothes as he closed the door behind him before walking across the room and sitting down beside her on the bed. Tracey couldn't move or speak as she watched him with a held breath that made her head spin; something had changed in Mr Burton. And she liked it.

It turned her on to think she could evoke such a change in this Adonis, and without even giving it much thought, she lunged at him. Pressing her soft lips to his in a rough kiss, her tongue licked across his lips, begging for admittance. His strong arms wrapped around her trim waist, lowering her onto the bed's soft embrace. When he opened, their tongues met in a fierce battle for dominance that made her toes curl and skin tingle.

The heated duelling of their tongues went on until their need for oxygen grew too great. Her thoughts foggy and panting hard, Tracey couldn't help flashing a toothy smile as she drank in Mark's equally dishevelled and aroused condition. Skin flushed and hair dishevelled, he had never looked so yummy.

Taking her devious little smile as a challenge, Mark flashed her that same grin, then seized her wrists and pinned her hands above her head. He straddled her hips, careful not put too much weight on her, before leaning down and covering her soft lips with his own. However, instead of the passion and ferocity like the last, this kiss was soft and tender, and he gently nibbled her top lip before tending to her lower with a soft suck that made her arch beneath him.

Never once did he make any move to deepen the kiss, instead he stocked her ardour with a gentle intimacy that was left to burn in the fires of her arousal.

"Oh! Oh please… Mr Burton!" Tracey tried to break free, needing more than this, desperate to at long last, fulfil all her wild fantasies. Though gentle, his hold was as firm as iron fetters around her wrists. She lacked the strength to overpower this man, so there she remained, firmly locked in his strong embrace while his lips teased her, sending her spiralling into hot, needy delirium.

Only when he had judged her thoroughly worked up did Mr Burton reclaim her mouth, his large hands brushing down her arms and spine to curl around her waist, crushing her against his hard warmth.

Whimpering under his savage intensity, Tracey clung to her friend's father as though her life depended on it, her fingers losing themselves in the softness of his hair as his tongue delved deep within her mouth. She could feel his hands running over her body, his every touch searing through her clothes, heat pooling in her centre. She sighed in delight when he cupped her buttocks and gave it a firm squeeze. Needing more, she slid her leg up to his thigh and over his hip, opening herself up to him and giving her better leverage. However, she couldn't contain herself when the immensity of his arousal pushed against her covered womanhood. She broke away to loose a long sweet gasp, her eyes nearly rolling, her head thrown back. It was too much, too good. "Mmm-Mr Burton!"

Delighting in her responsiveness, Mark trailed open-mouthed kisses along her jaw and down the slope of her neck to her collarbone, occasionally stopping to nip the sensitive skin and then sooth it with his tongue. All the while he gently stroked her abdomen, his fingers creeping up under her top, exploring the soft bounty beneath until he came to her breasts. With the pad of his thumb, he outlined the boundaries of her cleavage, every so often teasing the peak of a pebbled nipple. Smiling as he felt her arch into him, he licked his lips. *Time to kick things up a notch.*

All it took was a moment. A sudden jerk, the shriek of tearing fabric. He tore her top down the middle.

Surprised, Tracey squeaked as she was left bare to his gaze. Mark silenced any further protest with a kiss. There could be no resisting him now.

Pulling back, Mark almost licked his lips. *God... she's just gorgeous.* Tracey's breasts were full and firm but just large enough to fit in the palm of his hand, her flawless milky complexion accentuating her rosy nipples.

Taking his weight on his arm, Mark let his fingers wander over Tracey's curves, his hand closing over her breast, stroking and kneading it with a touch that made the girl gasp for breath every time he brushed her swollen peaks. His cock twitched at her eagerness, reminding him that she was not the only one in need of relief. Suddenly very aware of the awkward stiffness amassing at the base of his still-imprisoned cock- which happened to be growing more uncomfortable by the second- he bent down and took a pebbled bud between his lips, fiercely nipping her before soothing the sting with licks and sucks.

Moaning in agonised pleasure, Tracey lifted her hips and started rubbing against the man above her, all her self-doubt and nervousness forgotten. She didn't care anymore. All she wanted was this beast inside her, to feel him filling her, stretching her so completely she'd be ruined for other men. But still he continued to take his time, sucking first her right breast, then her left, before laying a trail of soft butterfly kisses down to her abdomen as he settled between her legs.

She all but screamed as a mini orgasm crashed over her when one large finger rubbed down the centre seam of her jeans, tracing along her swollen folds. "Please… Mr Burton?"

"Please what, Tracey?" Mark teased, sliding the offending finger up and down the garment's crotch a few times before fingering the fastenings. "What do you want sweetheart?"

"Do it?"

"Do. What?" He drew out each word with sultry emphasis before undoing the buttons. Catching the zipper between his teeth, he dragged it down, opening her up to his gaze.

"Stick your cock in me!" Tracey all but screamed it, hot, embarrassed, needy tears burning the corners of her eyes. But she didn't care, she needed this. Had needed it for so long. She didn't want to wait any more. She wanted him. "Fuck me!"

"Good girl." Mark removed her jeans and panties with a practised ease, tugging them both down and off her long willowy legs before casting them aside. Then he was once more hovering over her. Tracey had never felt so small and vulnerable, compounded by her own nakedness while he was still fully clothed. As much as she needed to feel him inside her, she wanted to ogle and worship his flesh, to see him in all his virile male glory-

Stars burst before her eyes as two fingers slipped inside her. Her whole body seemed to ripple around the very new and unexpected presence inside her. The teen's hips lifted from the bed to press his fingers deeper inside her hot channel. She moaned wantonly when they curled, rubbing a spot that made her thrash in ecstasy. But then his thumb began lavishing attention upon her clit, flicking and circling the way his tongue had teased her nipple and it all quickly became too much. He seemed to know exactly where to touch her, what she wanted before she did, and the tightness, the knot in her centre warned she would spill over the brink at any moment.

Only she didn't. Just when she was on the edge, an orgasm surging up to swallow her, he pulled his hand back.

"No!" Eyes widening, her whole body arched to follow him, and she threw a pleading hand out to try and drag him back between her legs, but it did no good. Grinning like the devil, Mr Burton brought his fingers up to her eyes, coated with juices, her juices, before licking them clean. *He's…tasting me.* The idea was as erotic as the show of his tongue slithering out to lap at each of his fingers in turn, and she suddenly longed to take those fingers into her mouth and suck them clean herself.

With her thoughts foggy and so close to release, she made no move to resist as the warmth of his breath washed across her abdomen, tickling her sex, before his tongue parted her folds and slid into her core, sending tendrils of pleasure through every nerve in Tracey's body.

"Mr Burton…Ah…Ah!" Tracey gasped, seizing fistfuls of his ebony mane, her hips rolling into his mouth when his teeth gently scraped her clit. "Oh God...urmph..." She could feel his tongue swirling around inside her, stroking and lashing her velvety inner walls as her nectar flowed into his open mouth. Yet it was the way he was staring up at her from between her legs, his eyes dark and burning, that she found the most carnal, pushing her closer and closer to her desired peak. And when he suddenly switched tact to suckling her small bundle of nerves with a low rumbling, something finally broke. "Uh-uh-uh-uh-oh…God! Ah-Ah-Ah…Cumming! I'm cumming!"

Then her vision turned white and melted away.

Chapter FOUR

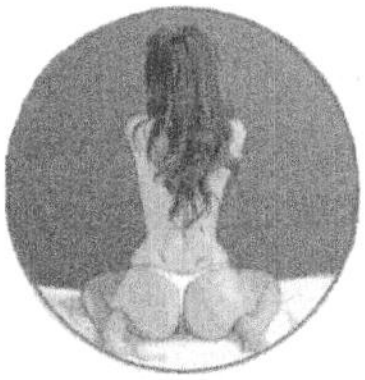

"Mmm... that was fantastic, sweetheart. You were amazing."

The words dragged her from a post-orgasm haze more effectively than a bucket of ice water. Blinking through the fog, Tracey awoke to find Amanda Burton standing over her. Her hair was down, a fall of soft and silky raven curls that tumbled more than halfway down her back. She'd changed out of her work clothes into a little silk robe that was tied at the waist and stopped much higher than her knees. It did nothing to hide her matching black stockings.

"Mrs Burton? What are you-"

"Shhh..." Amanda put a silencing finger to the girl's lips. "Just relax, the best is still to come."

Tracey obeyed and didn't utter a word, only gave a nervous nod, her heart fluttering at the prospect of what she had in store for her.

Amanda's smile broadened. "Good girl." Then she turned from her to face the base of the bed where her husband stood, shirtless, in all his male glory. Stepping in close, so he towered over her, she brought the hand that had silenced their newest toy up to brush feather soft along one bicep. She gave him a long look over, from toe to head, and then back down to linger on a point of immense interest. "Was it good for you too?"

Catching her hand in his, he brought it up to his mouth and kissed each of her fingers. "I was just having a little fun, love."

The kiss came hard and fast. His lips claiming her mouth with a singular passion, drawing her in deep, while his free arm hooked around her waist and spun her so that as he sat down on the edge of the bed, she landed in his lap.

She knew she shouldn't, that this night was for Tracey, but when her husband's tongue found her own, Amanda couldn't resist kissing back, wanting to absorb the sweetest sensations that only he could stir inside her with just the faintest touch. Drawing her in close, Mark hooked a finger through her robe, tugging the belt lose before slipping a hand through the folds to cup one of her breasts.

She gasped when he twisted her nipple, just hard enough for her to relish the cocktail of pleasure and pain, and then pushed him away. "No!"

He arched a brow. "Tease."

Breathing hard, Amanda had to resist the urge to kiss that cocky grin from his ridiculously handsome face. "Later, dear… this is for Tracey, remember."

At the mention of her name, Tracey could only nod her agreement, her eyes wide and mouth dry. She had seen other people kiss before, of course, but there had been something so raw and primitive between the Burtons. It was hot. She wanted more and watched on, unabashed, as Mrs Burton got to her feet and let her robe fall to the floor.

The sight of the older woman's naked bounty brought a tinge of pink to the girl's cheeks as she struggled to decide where to look. She also couldn't help feeling somewhat inadequate by comparison. Amanda's breasts were larger, her body better defined with a full sexy arse and long smooth legs that gave her a feline grace as she prowled up the bed on all fours. A stalking panther ready to pounce.

"Now let's get your lesson underway," Amanda teased in a breathy, sensual tone that sent tingles down Tracey's spine, before leaning in.

"Mrs Burton…" The kiss took Tracey completely off guard. It wasn't the chaste, almost motherly kiss she had grown accustomed to. No, this was hot and hungry, as the older woman practically devoured her with such demand that it would not be denied. It was such a strange feeling, but very pleasant and a little bit naughty. Tracey had never entertained thoughts about kissing another woman before, not even for experimentation purposes, but if this is what it was always like, she liked it. And with the sexual energy coursing through the room, she voluntarily succumbed to the older woman's wiles.

The kiss ended as quickly as it began, and Tracey's eyes fluttered open to find the Burton's sitting around her.

"Okay Tracey, this is how it's going to work," Amanda instructed in a very matter-of-fact tone, as though they were discussing something as every-day as the weather. Taking the teen's hand, she guided her off the bed so that her husband could lie down. "Mark and I are going to walk you through this every step of the way."

Tracey swallowed and nodded, her heart thumping loudly. She couldn't remember ever being so nervous.

"Just stay calm and play it by ear. Everything will come naturally, sweetheart," Amanda whispered soothingly, remembering all too well her own unease during hers and Mark's first night together. The thought brought a glint to her eye, a secret smile tugging at the corner of her lips. "I promise you're gonna love it."

Tracey nodded again, but the words did little to soothe the uneasy tightness in her lower belly and she suddenly longed for the floor to open beneath her. So, Mrs Burton gave her a gentle push and the matter was decided.

Half stumbling and half falling, she fell onto the bed to be swept up in Mark's arms and pulled atop a wall of hard male. She could feel his terribly aroused erection straining beneath her naked bottom. It felt enormous, much too big to ever fit inside her. Far from being a turn-off, however, the idea and the feel of the splendid specimen of masculinity beneath quickly rekindled her earlier fires. She wiggled her hips so his bulge nestled its way along her pelvis to the throbbing heat at the apex of her thighs. Swept up in the warmth of her arousal, she dipped her head to kiss her best friend's dad.

Matching her hunger, she felt him demanding entrance to her mouth. Not giving herself a chance to hesitate or second guess, she parted her lips and met his tongue greedily with her own. He tasted different, his masculine flavour spiced ever so slightly by a subtle heady essence. Her essence, she realised excitedly. She could taste herself. Excited by this discovery, she sucked his tongue greedily, growing almost drunk with ecstasy from their combined flavours, before suddenly pulling back and nipping a fiery trail down the exposed flesh of his neck.

Mark shuddered when she found the sensitive spot that joined his neck and shoulder and lashed it with her tongue, remembering how he had worked her body to that feverish pitch and knowing she was getting payback. It took every bit of willpower he possessed to keep his hands on the mattress and resist the urge to just throw the little minx to the bed and take her. *Payback's a bitch.*

In control or not, however, he couldn't stop himself from bucking against the tempting wench. Tracey suddenly moaned as his hardened cock rubbed up against her clit through his trousers.

"*Attagirl,*" Amanda purred, coming to stand around beside them where she could see them both clearly. "Do whatever feels natural, have fun with him but remember this is a marathon, not a race. So just take your time and learn what he likes." And just to prove her point, she took his earlobe between her lips and sucked.

"Oh!" Tracey gasped, her eyes widening at the feeling of Mark's body jumping beneath her and the weight of his cock grinding deliciously into her tender folds. Oh God, how she wanted to feel *that* inside her, stretching her to the point where even the slightest movement would make her see stars, to ride him into the sweet oblivion of *la petite mort*.

Amanda winked and licked her lips. "Understand?"

Nodding frantically, Tracey shifted to place her hands just below his collarbone and slid carefully off his lap to crouch between his legs. Careful to maintain as much skin to skin contact as possible, she laid a trail of licks and kisses down his hardened chest. A lifelong sportsman with a particular fondness for rugby, his body was littered with scars and she took special care to delicately lick each and every one before biting down on his flat nipples. As her mouth went lower, her fingers slid lightly down his arms to the waistline of his trousers. After popping open the last button, Tracey threw a hesitant glance at Amanda, who only nodded in encouragement.

"That's it, just take it slow. He's a big boy, but that just gives you more of him to play with." Seizing her hand by the wrist, she forced the girl to take the bull by the single, very large horn.

He was so thick that her fingers wouldn't meet as they closed around his velvet skin, just beneath his ridge. She could feel him pulsing within her grasp when she pressed her thumb on his sensitive tip. The spongy head was already slick and shiny with precum, and her thumb slid easily round and round his slit before, with Mrs Burton's guiding touch, giving him a wary stroke that drew a soft moan from his lips.

"Oh fuck…" He panted, his head momentarily falling back into the pillow and a fine sheen slowly forming across his upper body.

Her confidence growing, Tracey repeated the move, only a little longer this time, going from base to tip. She could feel him throbbing in her palm, his head swelling with each stroke, silently pleading for her. His thick musky scent made her mouth water. Turning her eyes up to meet his once more, she leaned in and took him into her mouth, her lips sliding over his crest.

"Easy, not so fast," Mrs Barton warned, putting a restraining hand on her shoulder. But it did no good.

It was a delicious sensation, holding the head of his cock with her lips. Mark's flavour spilt over her taste buds like thick syrup, fogging her brain. Remembering some of the more *interesting* clips she had found online that Cam had lent her, she slid both of her hands down to his taut, muscular thighs and began slowly bobbing her head. However, despite her enthusiasm, she quickly realised that she couldn't support his enormous cock without the aid of her hands. Moving one from his knee, she placed it at the base of his length and tried to take more of him, but her jaw began to ache before she got even half of him in.

And despite herself, she started to worry she wasn't doing it right. In the movies, there was never any doubt that the guy getting blown loved it, but while it was obvious from his light grunts and moans that Mr Burton was enjoying her attempts at a blow job, he just didn't seem to be enjoying it enough. She forced herself to try and take him all in.

"Tracey, no!"

A cough hit her like a tidal wave the moment the blunt tip smacked into the back of her throat. Then she couldn't breathe. It was too much, too big. Hot tears burned her eyes as her throat constricted, closing her airways so completely that panic ran like ice through her veins. The sensation was so overwhelming that she almost leapt off the bed, coughing violently, wheezing to catch her breath.

Amanda was already beside her, a hand rubbing circles over her back to calm her while she whispered soothing words. Like Tracey was a horse on the verge of bolting. "It's okay, sweetheart, that was just a bit too fast. It's okay…okay"

But it wasn't okay, not in the least.

Swallowing back tears of shame and embarrassment Tracey forced herself to speak. "Mrs Burton… I think… I think I need a little help?"

Amanda needed no explanation. In truth, she had been pleasantly surprised at how quickly Tracey had gone on her own. She had the general idea, experience would fill in the blanks. All she needed was guidance and a bit of *refining*.

"Okay, now, watch closely." She instructed, shifting to kneel between her husband's legs. "You have the right idea, but there's no need to rush, men like to be teased and worked up. The longer you keep him going, the stronger his orgasm will be." Demonstrating her point, Amanda bent down and began lightly kissing and licking his tip until Mark felt as if he was going to burst.

"Amanda…oh God…so good!" He gasped, his head rolling back in sheer pleasure as he felt her tongue dance across his velvety head before wrapping him in its warmth as ever so slowly, she began taking his cock into her mouth. There, Mark found he was incapable of words and his eyes visibly rolled back into his skull. The feeling of her tongue wrapped around him, massaging him into a delirium too great for him to stand. Struggling against the pleasure, he managed to moan "Amanda… more…more" before losing himself again as he felt his dick hit the back of her mouth.

Smiling inwardly at his desperate plea, Amanda slowly pulled away and flashed a sultry smile at Tracey. "Care to join me?"

Nodding, not trusting herself to speak, Tracey moved in beside the older woman. Together, they eyed his erect cock with obvious desire and began licking and sucking his member together. Mark, shocked by the sudden feeling of two mouths sliding over his sensitised flesh, was unsure of what to do with his hands. Grabbing fresh fistfuls of the bed sheets, he had to fight the urge to watch them as strands of curly gold and silky raven hair tickled his stomach and inner thighs.

Together they feasted on him.

Tracey eagerly followed the older woman's example, licking his shaft from the base to just below his tip, while Amanda busied herself with his balls, gently sucking one into her mouth. Slathering it with her tongue, she then released it, moving on to the other. She repeated this again and again until Tracey switched to kissing his tip, slowly taking him back into her mouth. His cock was so sensitive from being repeatedly brought to the brink, that Mark could feel even the slightest attention to his arousal. The feeling of teeth lightly scraping over his crown was almost more than he could stand. He so badly wanted to look at them, to watch Tracey's head bob up and down, his stiff member disappearing and reappearing through her luscious pink lips while his wife all but swallowed his testicles. Instead, his eyes were shut tight and his head was pressed back into the pillow.

He couldn't remember it ever being this good.

Swinging had never been his thing. When some of Amanda's friends had told her about *the lifestyle*, she had been enthralled with the idea. Mark had just assumed it was because all her friends were doing it, but he hadn't jumped at the thought of sleeping around. Amanda had known this almost as soon as she'd suggested it, but he had gone along with it just to make her happy. Much to his relief, his wife seemed far more interested in watching him shagging other women than welcoming other men between her legs. He never denied that he didn't mind being watched, but the sex had been lacking all the same. It had always felt more mechanical than passionate and he'd never really been into it, just going through the motions. It had been nothing like this.

"Oh fuck! Mmm -yeah just like- oh shit, I'm going to cum!" He cried, his tone guttural, as the pleasure grew so intense, he was pushed over the brink.

Tracey heard the desperation in his tone. She knew what was about to happen and it filled her with such a feeling of pride and conquest to know that she had done this to him. She wasn't ready to swallow though. That was a step too far out of her comfort zone.

"Don't you dare," Amanda hissed, a wild glint flashing in her eyes as she seized a fistful of the girl's hair, forcing her down and his cock to slide all the way into her mouth. "Come on, swallow every drop."

Eyes widening in panic, Tracey tried to resist, but it was already too late. She swallowed instinctively as the first shot of Mr Burton's cum hit the back of her throat, filling her mouth with his thick salty cream. Oblivious in his release, Mark's hips rolled as he rode his climax.

"That's it baby, isn't she such a good little cock-sucker?" Amanda urged her husband on, the throbbing in her clit growing stronger as she felt the resistance ebb out of Tracey. "Yeah, give her all your cum."

"So…so good," Mark panted, dark spots dancing before his eyes. Fuck, he hadn't cum that hard in years.

Chapter FIVE

Totally into it, Tracey licked Mark's cock clean with ravenous hunger, like she was licking melting ice cream on a hot summer day. It wasn't a particularly sweet or pleasant flavour, but there was something about its saltiness that grew on her as she drank every drop he had to give.

"Good girl" Amanda praised, letting the girl up while assessing her husband. Reeling from the force of his delayed release, Mark lay breathless on the bed, but he was still half hard and ready to go again. Capable, she decided, but nowhere near ready for what she had in mind.

Amanda turned and kissed Tracey full and hard and with all the raw sexual energy that the night had left sizzling through her core. She tasted as sweet as ever, like strawberries and cream, seasoned with Mark's saltiness. The memory that her mouth had been wrapped around her husband's cock just moment's ago excited her all more,

Taken by surprise, the girl was motionless at first, then the older woman's tongue found hers and reality caught up. She squeaked in surprise, her body stiffening, but Amanda pulled her in close. She abandoned Tracey's lips in favour of capturing a pink nipple with her tongue. Already madly aroused, Tracey arched and tossed her head back in a cascade of gold, moaning long and low as they tumbled back into the bed's embrace.

"Mmm… Such beautiful tits." Amanda purred, sucking and tonguing the ripe bud. Tracey's fervour grew.

"No-oh! Don't say that, it's embarisi-oh there, right there!"

"Yeah, you like that? Want more?"

"Yes… oh God, oh God!" The whole world seemed to burst with light, heat, and pleasure as Mrs Burton's finger slid into her, curling up to tease her g-spot while the pad of her thumb manipulated her clit. "...Feels so good… please, more, I want more!"

"Don't worry sweetheart," Amanda cooed, glancing across the bed to Mark. He was transfixed, his cock rapidly returning to full mast. She grinned inwardly. "I'll give you more" And she pulled away.

Tracey felt close and her eyes snapped open. She immediately made to grab Mrs Burton's retreating hand, desperate to bring those fingers back. She'd fuck herself on them if that was what it took for her to get off. Amanda just batted her hand away and settled herself between the girl's thighs.

"Be patient sweetie, I promise you're going to love this." With a seductive smile, she pulled the girl's right leg over her left, while hooking her own over hers. "And I think you can call me Amanda now."

"Mrs Bur- Amanda, what are you-?" The question died as their pussies kissed.

It was an odd sensation, all friction and heat, but one that elected moans from them both. So she might tease her husband just that little bit longer, Amanda rocked their bodies together, the position just right for their clits to grind together.

"Oh fuck!" Tracey moaned, arching her back and crying out in ecstasy, the pleasure hitting her like the waves of a tempest, crashing over her fast and hard. "Yes…fuck me...fuck me...oh God...yes!"

"Uh... Fuck.... alright sweetheart…" Amanda groaned, delighting in the hot shivers rippling through her, the circles of her hips growing more forceful. "I'll fuck you...uh…now…cum for me...oh!"

Tracey couldn't stand it. It was too intense, too hot. Her body felt like fire, tongues of white flame spreading out from her wet and throbbing cunt. She was so close.

But it wouldn't come. She could practically feel herself dangling on the edge. "I can't!" She whimpered.

"Oh baby, yes you can." Amanda pressed, rising to close the gap between them and attack the hollow of the girl's neck with licks and nips while grinding their clits together. "Let it all out so Mark can see, he's watching. Let my husband see that pretty face of yours as I make you cum. Then he's going to take your precious virginity and make you cum on his big yummy cock. Go on, cum! Cum! Cum!"

Mr Burton. She knew she shouldn't look, but Tracey couldn't help herself. Mr Burton was watching, and it made her belly flutter. He was wreathed in shadow and light, dark and deliciously dangerous, his eyes burning bright as he watched her with a predatory hunger, his cock standing tall. He wasn't touching himself and that excited her. *All this for me.*

"Mr Burton, I-I…Oh fuck, fuck! I'm cumming! I'm cumming!"

"Attagir- Oh shit! Yes! Yes, right there, oh! Yes! I'm cumming too!" Amanda followed almost immediately, pushed over the brink and into oblivion.

Relaxing into their simultaneous releases, the two women slipped into a serene afterglow.

Tracey felt like she was floating in a warm bath and just staying awake became a chore as her eyes grew heavy and all the cares of the world seemed to float away. If this was a dream, then she hoped she would never wake up.

Through half-lidded eyes, she watched Amanda slowly rise to her knees on shaky legs and manoeuvre around to sit beside her husband and whisper something in his ear. He nodded and then she was gone. Mark was looming over her.

He scooped her up as if she weighed nothing and placed her gently down at the head of the bed. She felt the mattress sink under his weight as he crawled up the length of her body.

"There's no going back after this, Tracey," His voice was gruff, but when he cupped her chin his touch was gentle. "Are you sure this is what you want?"

Even now, he was still concerned for her, but the thought of him stopping had her arms snaking up around his neck. She arched, opening her gates. "Mmm… I've never been so sure." She husked, rolling the heat of her moist arousal along his cock. "Mr Burton, please, *fuck me."*

He nodded, easing forward. Tracey's head rolled back onto her shoulders, her lips parting and her eyes falling shut as his broad crest slid slowly inside-

A bolt of pain ran up Tracey's spine as she felt the excruciating pop of her virginity.

"It…It…hurts…" she whimpered, fighting back tears and digging her nails into his back so hard that trickles of blood ran down his skin.

"Relax…sweetheart," Mark mouthed into her hair, fisting the sheets against the urge to fuck her as her inner walls bore down on him. He needed to wait, to let her adjust, but fuck she was tight. "The pain will pass. It's better this way, just like ripping off a plaster. Now you just need to relax."

Tracey could only nod and cling to him, dragging in deep breaths as the pain began to fade. The pain turned into pleasure and Tracey felt herself floating away.

Torn between torturous pleasure and exquisite agony, Mark could only grit his teeth against the desire to cum right then and there. "God, your pussy feels so good."

His words were anaesthesia. Tracey wanted more of him, wanted to feel him move inside of her, pounding her, fucking her to insanity, the heat of his seed filling her to the brim...

She couldn't stand it. Moving her hips, she began to grind against the base of his shaft, making them both moan and draw in a shuddering breath.

The thrill she got from their union was breath-taking. Tracey eagerly tried to take more, but Mark's hands trailed down to cup her bum, his powerful grip holding her still.

"Mr… Mr Burton…please…I want…" She moaned, her body's need for him growing almost frenzied as he rolled his hips. He was being gentle, lightly touching her, teasing. No, this wasn't what she wanted.

"What do you want sweetheart? Go on, tell me…"

"Fuck me." She growled, legs crossing over his buttocks. "Now!"

He smiled, then thrust down as she moved to meet him, forcing her to take another two inches of him.

"Mr…Burton…" Tracey gasped, all defiance melting away as he withdrew almost completely from her depths. She felt infected with an empty feeling as he pulled back before finally thrusting home. "Oh…oh God! I'm gonna burst! Yes, Yes! Don't stop, don't ever stop... I want more. Make me scream!"

"Don't worry sweetheart, you're about to get the fuck of your life." Her pussy was slick and tight, her inner muscles clenching around him. He pulled away before returning fast and hard, slamming into her, every inch of him filling her.

"Oh fuck…Fuck me, fuck me!"

"Yeah? You like that Tracey?" he teased, thrusting into her harder, faster. "You like getting fucked by your best friend's dad?"

"Yes…Yes… your cock feels so good, like it's splitting me in half!" she moaned, every thrust hitting deeper than the last. "Oh my God! Don't stop! Don't Stop…"

Mark complied. Holding nothing back, he ravaged her sweet young body with wild abandon, working his cock inside her tight folds with urgency. She was beautiful, her naked body dancing to his rhythm.

A high-pitched cry escaped her lips as Mark thrust deep, grazing her g-spot. She cried out in a frenzied passion, her nails raking his skin. Tracey was losing control.

Mark could feel both of their releases drawing close and was trying his best to keep his under control. Tracey needed to cum first. He reached down to where their bodies were joined and began playing with her sensitive clit, rubbing it gently with the pad of his thumb.

The tidal wave of her orgasm crashed over her with colossal force, sending her senses into overdrive. She convulsed and contracted around his throbbing cock, her cream coating his stiff shaft as he pounded her straight through one orgasm, and into a second. He let out a low grunt of pleasure as he erupted inside her.

They stayed like that for a few minutes, basking in the afterglow of their respective orgasms before he wrapped his arms around her and drew her close as he rolled onto his back.

Amanda sat down beside them on the bed. "Havin' fun?"

Tracey giggled girlishly while Mark shot his wife a half-smile. "You could say that."

"Good." Amanda matched his smile, then bent to whisper in Tracey's ear. "Now that you're a woman, sweetheart, how about celebrating with your first threesome?"

“Really?” Surprised, Tracey weakly tried to sit up, but her jelly arms wobbled so dangerously, she could only manage a slight tilt of her chin. “But I don’t…I mean…what…”

“Just move over sweetie, there’s nothing to it,” Amanda assured before climbing over the pair and sitting against the headboard. She opened her legs, revealing her glistening folds and, with a kinky smile playing across her lips, beckoned the girl closer with her finger.

Mark could only watch dry-mouthed as Tracey climbed off him and crawled between his wife’s thighs. Amanda then motioned for him to join them. Smiling to himself, he rose and slid into place behind Tracey.

Placing her head next to Amanda’s slick sex, Tracey buried her face into Amanda’s heat, remembering how Mark had devoured her own.

"Yeah… Oh God Tracey… Oh... yeah… just like that...." Amanda moaned, rolling her hips and grinding her pussy into the girl’s face. At the same time, Mark grabbed Tracey's waist and lined himself up to enter her. Looking up, the couple’s eyes met, and he gave her a wicked smirk before he teasingly slid the tip of his cock up her still tingling and oversensitive pussy, to her ass.

“Mmm…decisions, decisions…” He pondered.

Smiling back, Amanda reached forward with both hands. She grabbed and spread Tracey’s cheeks, opening the girl up to her lover. “Here dear, fuck her virgin ass.”

Tracey looked up, her eyes glazed with uncertainty. “But Mrs Bur- Amanda, doesn't it…? Isn't that supposed to hurt?” She asked.

“Don't worry honey,” Amanda said, smiling down at her. “Mark’s very good at anal. It’ll sting at first, but I’m going to make sure you enjoy every second.” She twisted them around and positioned herself underneath her.

Smirking as he watched his wife devour their lover, Mark moved back into position behind them. Holding Tracey's hips still, he pressed the tip of his cock into her rear entrance.

"Whatever you do Tracey, don't tense." He warned before moving forward, pressing home. The admittance to her rear made Tracey's whole-body arch in simultaneous pain and ecstasy as Amanda greedily tongued her clit.

Allowing her a few moments to get accustomed to the sensation, Mark began to slowly work his length back and forth, sliding that little bit deeper inside her as he did. "Shit… so tight, so… tight…"

Unfortunately, this was a new sensation that even Amanda's incredible oral skills couldn't disguise. Tracey was forced to squeeze her eyes shut as sharp stabs of pain ripped through her petite body. However long fingers quickly replaced that pain with pleasure as they began squeezing the nub of her clit, testing it like a ripe grape while she tongued her folds. Tracey reciprocated.

"Oh, Mr Burton…" Tracey moaned, her head starting to spin. "Please… it feels… good… so good. More… I want more. Please!" Then she buried her face between Amanda's thighs, locking her lips around her clit, sucking wantonly.

"I knew she'd love taking it up her butt- oh! Yes, suck it, sweetheart, that's it, mmm" Amanda managed between moans. "Give it to her baby, fuck her, fill her tiny ass with your big dick!"

Hearing the pair's demands, Mark began to vigorously fuck the teen, slamming his flesh into her, filling her little butt with his cock with every thrust. Tracey moaned with delight as his hard cock filled her arse over and over, making her small body rock and sway to his undeniable rhythm.

The room was quickly filled with the trio's moans, their cries of pleasure working to drive each other to their own peak. It wasn't long before Tracey felt another earth-shattering climax brewing from the couple's affections.

Her body over-burdened by the taste of Amanda and the feel of Mark. Tracey's core tingled, and her body throbbed as Mark drove into her harder and faster, pushing her over the edge.

"Uh…oh God! Mrs-Mrs Burton! …I'm…I'm cumming!" Tracey groaned around Amanda's clit, pushing her to her own climax.

Mark's head lolled back as a series of low, guttural moans escaped his mouth. It was too much. He thrust into Tracey as deep as he could before releasing a howl as he came, filling her tight bowels with his hot seed in the rush of another powerful orgasm. The sensation consumed her in an instant and Tracey's world went black.

Coming down from their high, the lovers relaxed in each other's company, riding the remnant waves of their orgasms. It took some time for Amanda and Mark to realise that Tracey had passed out after her third orgasm.

"Thank you, baby," Amanda murmured, snuggling into her husband, enjoying the heat he gave off as she listened to the deep rumble of his heartbeat.

"Oh…What for, my love?"

With a knowing smile, she leant up and kissed her cheek. "For doing this, for Tracey. I know it couldn't have been easy for you."

"It was nothing honey." He grinned and kissed her forehead. "Anytime."

Don't forget to Keep in Touch

You can find the Lord of Lust on **Facebook**, **Twitter**, **Instagram**, **Goodreads** and **Bookbud**. He loves chatting with his readers and 100% approves of stalking.

Be Sure to join his **Reader Group**, The Sweet Temptations - https://www.facebook.com/groups/580219985516975

Check out his **Website** – lmmountford.com, to learn more about his books, upcoming releases, and public appearances. And while there, don't forget to subscribe to his **Newsletter**, where you will receive a free book daily from best sellers and newbie authors alike!

Also by
L.M. Mountford

Age is just a number, and this collection of sinfully steamy age-gap romances will prove it...

The Lord of lust has done it again and in this anything but sweet, four book Box Set, full of forbidden Silver Foxes and sassy Cougars, he proves that age is no boundary to love, or lust.

A collection of hot and orgasmic stories by The Lord of Lust
Do you love hard men, strong women, sizzling chemistry and erotic scenes that make Fifty Shades of Grey look like five shades of beige?
Well, here you go...
7 Books, 7 hard and rugged men, 7 sizzling page turners that will have you devouring every word from start to finish...

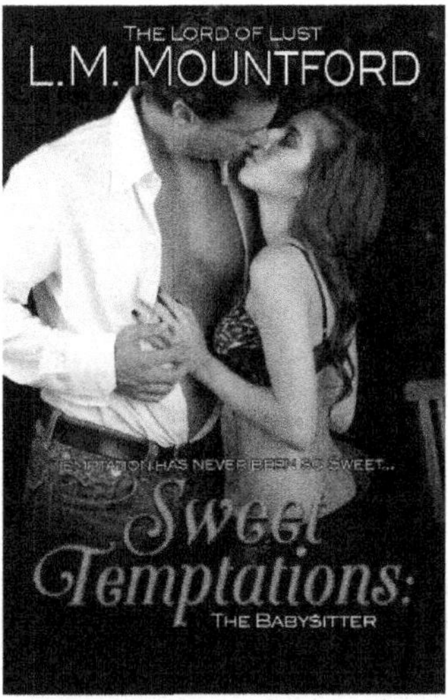

Temptation has never been so sweet...

Richard Martin's life was only just starting to come back together, then **she** opened the door in that damn little black robe that shows off plenty of leg, and every curve.

She, Rebecca Blaire, the girl from downstairs. His babysitter.

She's everyman's fantasy, a big doe-eyed nymph, as beautiful as she is innocent.

Forbidden fruit in every sense of the word.

And she desperately needs his help, before her abusive father comes home and beats her black and blue.

Richard knew he should just walk away. It wasn't any of his business really, and nothing good could come from going through that door, but then...

Some temptations are just too sweet to resist.

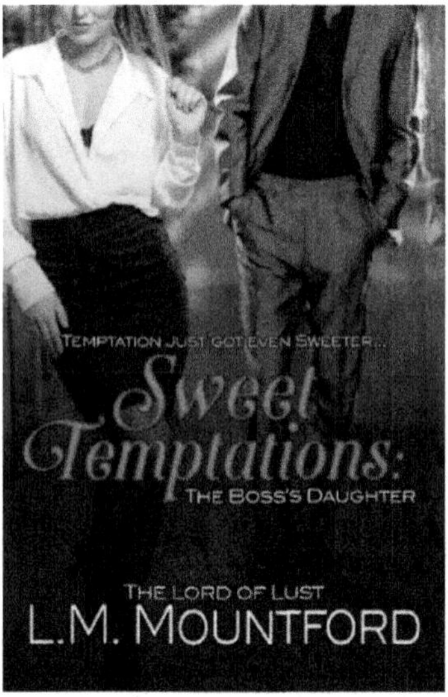

He thought his temptations were over, but they were only just beginning…

Until last week, Richard Martin was just another middle-aged guy. Married to a wife he loved, father to a son he adored, stuck in a dead-end job, just counting the days go by…

Then everything changed.

He made a mistake.

Now to save his marriage, he's going to have to pay the price.

There's just one problem, Scarlet Holmes.

His Supervisor.

She loves to play games with her staff and now, seeming very aware of his little secret, she wants to play a game.

And she always gets what she wants.

Because she just so happens to be The Boss's Daughter.

Temptation at its Sweetest…

Book 1: The Babysitter

Book 2: The Boss's Daughter

Sweet Temptations: books 1&2 are sizzling tales that break all the rules and combine lust, seduction and temptation. Loaded with drama and heat, this boxset will ignite your ereader and leave you panting for more.

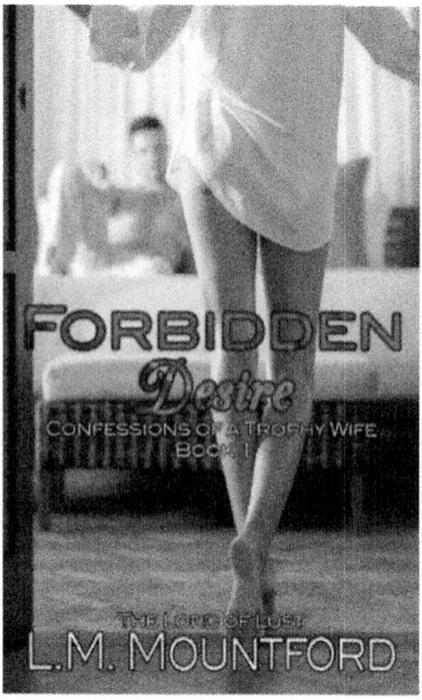

To all the rest of the world, Elizabeth Clarke has it all.

A successful husband. A beautiful home. And now a son off to university. She is a perfect housewife with the perfect life.

It's a lie.

Her husband is a lying, drinking philanderer who hates her as much as she loathes him. Her home is beautiful, but empty, nothing more than a gilded cage to keep her trapped in a world she never wanted.

That is, until he came back into town.

Hugh Becket.

Her son's best friend. He's hot, young, and so forbidden.

Elizabeth knows she should stay away, but when the devil comes knocking on her door in the middle of the night, what's a poor neglected trophy wife to do?

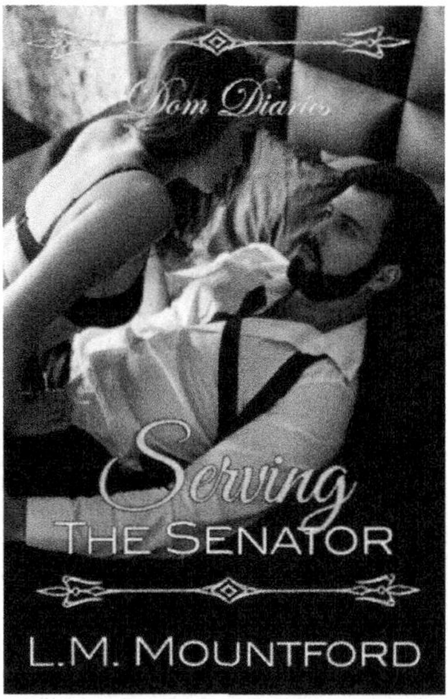

He is my Hades

I'd played the role of a goddess, bound and chained for the service of mortals.

He freed me.

He freed me, unchained me and taken me to his underworld, his dark realm where he'd brought out all my forbidden and secret desires.

And now I'm his.

His attendant. His servant…

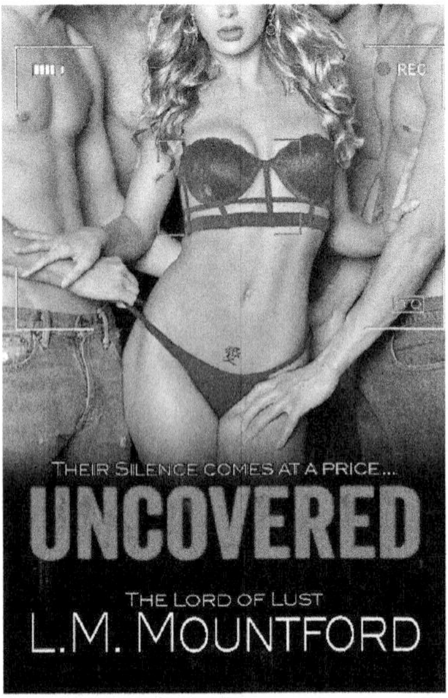

When Mina returns for her stepbrother's 21st birthday, she thinks her days of lusting after him are over. Caught up in the heat and passion of the moment, she is stunned to find them back in bed together; their feelings clearly far from resolved. Haunted by her desire, Mina now has another problem… she must head down a path of lust and desire; torn between the dark delights of the handsome bad boy down the street and her adorable stepbrother who has always been there for her. Can she confront the truth she has long tried to bury? How far will she go to save the one she wants, but knows she can never truly have?

As an underworld princess, daughter to the boss of mob bosses all along the east coast, Sophie's life was a gilded cage.
A prison of gold and silk…
That is until Luke stepped into her life.
A scrapper from the back streets, who had risen from among the ranks to stand in her shadow.
Luke, her bodyguard, and her secret lover.
Their destinies were never meant to cross, but they had. It was impossible, forbidden, but they couldn't resist…
Now their one reckless night has become a desperate fight for their lives.

I may have been a bad influence on her when we were kids, but this new side of her is going to ruin me...

They were the best of friends. Then they shared a night of passion and in the morning she was gone and Alex has spent years trying to move on.

But then an email arrives out of the blue and suddenly he finds himself boarding the first plane bound for Australia with nothing but his passport and an overnight bag. He's no idea what he'll do, or he's going to say, but one thing's for sure...

He's not going home without her.

Together in Sydney is a Second Chance Romance full of steamy scenes and bad language. It's only recommended for readers 18+. No cliffhanger. Guaranteed HEA!

Sooner or later, the thirst always wins…
After a thousand years, Lucian had given up any interest in the world. His only concern that night was finding his next drink, preferably from a flavoursome twenty-something with loose morals and no expectations. Then he saw her…
Kate is just a girl from the country, who came to the city with her brother to find a life away from their parents' car crash. That is until the police came knocking on her door one morning and ripped her new life apart.
Now she has nothing and no one, with only one on her mind...
When these worlds collide, and the things that go bump in the night come calling, can these two mend the rifts in each other and give them what they need?

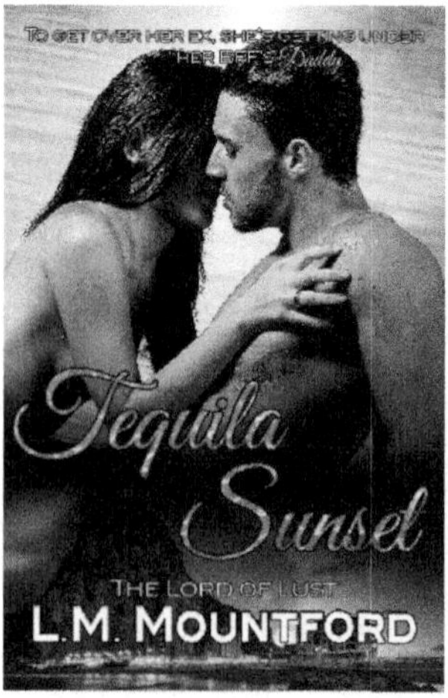

'I'm sorry Cassy, but you're just too boring for me,'
That was the story of Cassandra's life.
She was always that girl. The curvy plain jane. She was fine with it, right up until her hot bad boy ex threw it in her face before walking out of her life. Leaving her depressed and reeling, doubting everything about herself and her future…
So her best friend has spirited her away to her family's Gibraltar Vila for a little fun in the sun, some much needed girl time, and a whole lot of boys.
There's just one problem.
David, her best friend's recently divorced dad also happens to be staying at the villa. And he's no boy...

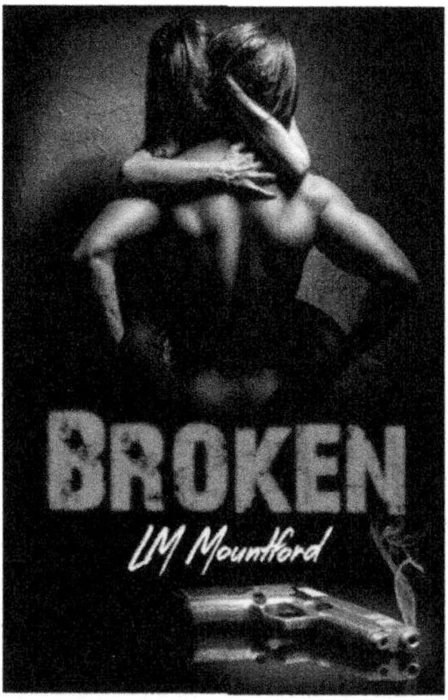

Vickey Romano is the girl with a secret you don't want to bring home to mum.

Beautiful, haunted, and on the run, she works a string of temp jobs and never lets anyone get too close. Until that is, she meets Jake. The living definition of dark and dangerous, he tells her nothing about himself, keeps a SIG P226 in his bedside table and can make her go weak-kneed with just a word.

She knows she should stay away, he has her caught in his web and she's helpless to resist.

All she can do is hope her past doesn't kill him in the process...

Broken is a hard and gritty Dark romance. The opening in the Broken Heart Series, it balances sex and violence on a knife edge and will draw you down a web of mystery with every page.

They were the very poster children for the boy and girl next door, if a couple of streets apart.

Friends for longer than forever. They'd walked to school together. He'd protected her from the bullies when they teased her about her glasses. She'd tended to his cuts and bruises when he fell. He pushed her to try new things. She snuck looks at him when he wasn't looking.

All her life, Faye had loved Terry, but he was oblivious. He's her best friend, her closest friend, but he's oblivious and now he has a Girlfriend. All day long, she has to watch them together and it's killing her. She wants him, all of him, but he's taken. So, instead, she wants one night. Just once, one night, between friends.

One night, just once...

Printed in Great Britain
by Amazon

37527762R00037